THE DARK SECRET OF THE OUIJA

By Terry Ann Modica

Illustrated by Al Bohl

A BARBOUR BOOK

TO *my children,*
David and Tammy,
for their special help with this book.

THE DARK SECRET
OF THE OUIJA

"THEY'RE WRONG!"

1

"They're wrong! They're wrong!" Jenny Seker screamed as she slammed the door to her bedroom. Its loud ka-thump shut out the chatter of the grown-ups downstairs. Leaning against the door, Jenny let out an angry groan and tried to hold back the burning tears. "They just can't be right about Daddy."

She missed him terribly. Her room, though crowded by the twin beds, twin desks, and matching dressers, seemed so empty. Her father had painted this furniture long ago; it needed new paint now.

Jenny strode around her sister's bed to get to her own dresser and the picture of her father. The eight-inch by ten-inch photo sat tall among the hair brushes and various souvenirs of her fourteen years, glistening in its gold-colored frame.

She lifted it gently and studied the image of the smiling, dark-haired man. Her mother often said that Jenny had her father's smile. Her wavy, shoulder-length hair was a few shades lighter than his, but she had the same hazel eyes. In the photo, Dad seemed to be asking what the problem was.

"I know it can't be true what Uncle Jack said about you," she said. "The accident was *not* your fault. You were not drunk." She paused. "Uncle Jack must hate you or something, 'cause Mom never blames you for the accident. And she *never* says you drank too much."

Indeed, Jenny's mother rarely spoke of the accident at all. All she told her two daughters was, "Just remember your dad loved us all very much, and he still does."

From time to time over the past six years since, Jenny had overheard relatives talking about her father's death. They called him a drunk who had caused the Tragedy. They would always call it "the Tragedy," and then stare at each other as if there were some hidden, unspeakable horror.

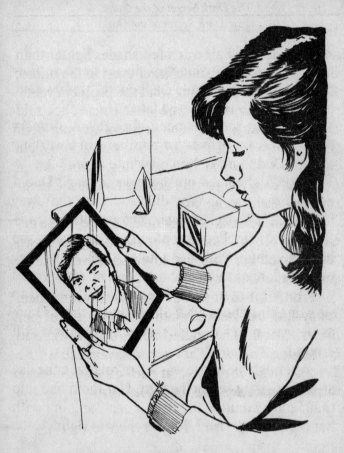

"The accident was not your fault"

"They're just making up stories because they don't know what really happened," Jenny said, touching the glass-covered face.

What did really happen, though? A slippery road? A crazy driver in another car swerving toward Dad to make him plow into a tree?

Jenny sighed and brushed away a tear. "Dad, I miss you so much. Why did God take you away from me?" She sighed again. "I love you."

As she clutched the photo to her chest, she heard laughter from the adults. Apparently, they were no longer talking about her dad. How could they forget him so easily? Jenny never wanted to stop thinking about Dad. She believed that as long as he was in her thoughts, he was somehow still around.

Although the house was full of relatives, the day after Christmas seemed empty. Her mom had said that Jenny would feel better if she hung out with her cousins and sister. Maybe she was right.

"Why did God take you away?"

Jenny slowly set the photo back in its place. When she went down to the living room, she paused by the Christmas tree. Jenny hunted for a small gift in blue wrapping paper. It was nearly hidden by bits of red and green paper and a few opened presents. Jenny glanced around the room to check if anyone could see her. Everyone seemed to be in the kitchen. Good! She bent down to pick it up.

This was her present to Dad. Every year since his death, she'd written him a note, wrapped it, and left it under the tree.

"Ha-ha-ha!" The mocking laughter came from behind her. It was Samantha, her scrawny little sister.

"Shut up, you twerp!" Jenny scolded.

Samantha formed a gloating smile on her freckled face. "That's a dumb thing to do. A present for Daddy!"

"I said shut up!"

"Ha-Ha-Ha!"

Samantha eyed the gift. "Do you think his ghost is going to come get it? What's in it, anyway?" Samantha grabbed it out of Jenny's hand.

"Give that back!"

Samantha ran toward the stairs. "I'm going to see what's in it."

"No! Don't open it! I'll tell Mom." Jenny moved closer, but Samantha jumped up a couple of stairs.

"No you won't, because you don't want anyone to know about this present."

She had a point. Jenny lunged at the gift. Sam snatched it away and dashed up the stairs. Jenny ran after her. Sam disappeared behind the bedroom door. As Jenny's hand reached the doorknob, she heard the lock click. The knob refused to turn.

"Let me in! You can't lock me out of my own room."

"I'm opening the present now."

"No! I swear I'll scratch your eyes out if you do."

Lunging for the gift

Silence was Sam's response.

"Please, Sam, don't." Jenny tried to force the doorknob. Tears of anger and embarrassment wet her cheeks. "Don't."

"'Dearest Daddy,'"Sam's voice quoted. "'I hope you're having a merry Christmas where you are. Do they have Christmas parties in Heaven?'"

Samantha laughed. "Right. Good one, Jen."

She continued reading. "'I miss you very, very, very much. Why did you have to die?'" Her voice grew quiet. "'Is it true what some people say about you, that you killed yourself by driving drunk? I don't believe that. But I want proof the accident was not your fault, so I can tell them all how wrong they are. I wish you could give me a message or some sign about what really happened. Say Happy Birthday to Jesus for me. I love you always.'"

Both girls were silent for some long moments. "I hate you," Jenny whispered.

The door slowly opened. Sam shoved the box and letter into Jenny's hand. "That's a dumb

"I hate you"

present," she said. She darted for the stairs and the safety of the group in the kitchen.

Jenny kicked the door. "I hate you, Samantha," she said through clenched teeth. "Daddy, why aren't you here to make her be nice to me?" She looked at his photo and imagined smashing it. The thought horrified her. She couldn't be angry at him. She missed him too much. But if the relatives were right about him, she'd have good reason to be angry.

She headed for the bathroom and threw the gift in the trash. "Sam's right," she said. "It *is* a dumb present." To shake off the feeling of loneliness, she decided to call her best friend, Carol Astrey. She walked into her mother's room to use the phone.

At the sound of her friend's voice, Jenny began to pour out her hurts. She complained about Samantha and reported the unkind things Uncle Jack had said.

"And Christmas is supposed to be a time of loving one another and being kind," she finished.

"Hello, Carol"

"Hah!" Carol said. "Not when you have brothers and sisters! You should see it around here."

"At least we have each other."

"Friends for life."

"So what did you get for Christmas?"

"Some clothes and jewelry and junk like that. Some games. Oh! Guess what one of those games is. A Ouija board!"

"Isn't that a fortune-telling game? What's it like?"

"It's awesome! Two people put their hands on a pointed thing that moves around the board to spell out answers to questions."

"What kinds of questions?"

"Any questions."

"Did you try it? Does it really work?"

"Yeah, I played it with a couple of my sisters. It works, but the answers aren't always, you know, amazing. I think our own minds control it."

"It's awesome!"

"What if your mind doesn't already know the answer?"

"You want to try it?"

"Sure. I have the perfect question to ask it!"

"What is it?"

"This might be the answer to my prayers. Maybe God will use it to tell me what really happened when my father died."

"I have the perfect question for it"

"Spookiness is half the fun"

2

Carol Astrey closed the lavender curtains in her bedroom to darken the room. She turned her slightly plump face toward Jenny. "This'll help us get in the mood," she said. Then she joined her friend on the carpeted floor.

"Don't you think this game is spooky?" Jenny asked as Carol placed the Ouija board between them. "I mean, what if the answers don't come from our own minds?"

Carol flipped her long, blond hair out of her face and grinned. "Spookiness is half the fun of it!"

"I suppose."

Jenny had never seen one of these games before, although she'd heard about it from kids at school. The board was printed with the alphabet and numbers and the words *yes* and *no* in fancy lettering. A picture of a fortune-teller with a crystal ball was in the middle of the board. Carol placed something that looked like a plastic triangle on short legs on the picture.

"This is a planchette," she explained. "It'll point to the letters to spell out the answers. Touch it very lightly with your fingertips. Don't push it. Just wait for the planchette to move by itself."

The two friends sat facing each other, touching the pointer. The pose struck Jenny as funny. She giggled. Carol giggled, too.

"Stop it!" Carol took a deep breath. "We have to be in the right mood, or it won't work. What question to you want to ask?"

Jenny cleared her throat and tried to wipe the smile from her face. She knew that laughter came from nervousness. But why should this make her nervous? The Ouija board was just a game. "You go first," she said.

"Okay. I'll ask, umm, does Mark like me?"

Jenny forced herself to picture Mark Talbot, the hunk from English class. She nearly freaked when she felt the pointer move.

"Does Mark like me?"

"You're pushing it!" she accused Carol.

"Shhh! I am not. I'm hardly touching it."

The pointer traveled very slowly to the word *yes*.

Carol let out a squeal of delight. "All right!"

Jenny took her hands off the pointer and grinned at her friend. "I wonder if Mark knows he likes you."

Carol's round cheeks blushed. "It's your turn, now."

"But what makes the planchette move? My fingers were barely touching it."

"I don't know. Maybe our fingers do push it, but in such a small way we can't feel ourselves doing it. Ask your question."

They put the pointed back in the middle of the board and placed their fingertips on it. Jenny stared at it. "How did my dad really die?"

The planchette didn't move.

"Come on, Ouija board," Jenny whispered. "Use your power to give me the answer."

"All right!"

"It's starting!" Carol said, grinning.

Jenny barely breathed as she waited.

Slowly, the pointed headed for the "A." Then "C." Carol announced each letter.

"A-C-C-I-D-E-N-T. Accident!"

"Yeah, big deal," Jenny said. "I know it was an accident. But how did it happen?"

"Okay, let's ask it that," Carol said as she returned the pointer to the center.

This time it spelled out *car.*

"Great. I knew that, too." Jenny shoved the planchette across the board. "This game's not helping me."

"I have an idea," Carol said.

"What?"

"Maybe we have to do this where there's some memories of your father. At your house."

"Let's go!"

A walk down several blocks of slushy sidewalks took them to Jenny's house. Before they could go upstairs to Jenny's room, however, they had to say

Walking to Jenny's

hello to all the relatives. Jenny's mother told her to introduce Carol.

As Jenny made the introductions, Aunt Sadie spotted the Ouija board under Carol's arm. "Are you planning to use that?" She gave the girls a sharp look.

"We might." Jenny shrugged.

Aunt Sadie shook her head. "I've heard some pretty bad things about that game. People say they talk to spirits with it."

"Ahh, we're not going to do that," Jenny said.

"Yeah," Carol added. "The answers only come from our minds."

"Humph!" Aunt Sadie replied.

Jenny bowed out of the kitchen with Carol close behind. When they entered Jenny's room, they pulled shut the door and curtains.

"Wouldn't it be awesome if we could talk to my father's spirit?" Jenny mused. "Maybe Aunt Sadie was right about using the Ouija board to contact spirits."

"Are you planning to use that?"

"Maybe. That's *really* spooky. I don't think it's possible, though."

"Yeah. Well, let's play." Jenny jumped onto her bed, smoothed out the blanket and motioned for Carol to set up the board.

When all was ready, Jenny stared at her father's picture and concentrated. "What caused Daddy's car accident?" she asked.

The pointer didn't budge at first, but finally it started heading for the letters. D-R-U-N-K.

"Drunk? Who was drunk? Not my dad."

"Other person," Carol read.

"There was another person!" Jenny clapped her hands. "Daddy was killed by another driver who was drunk! Of course!"

Carol eyed her, frowning. "Where do you think that answer came from?"

"I don't know."

"It came from your mind. That's the answer you wanted to hear."

"There was another person?"

Jenny glared at Carol. "Do you think my dad killed himself, the way Uncle Jack does? I thought you were my friend."

"You know I am."

"And you should know I always want to know the truth, whatever it is."

"Then where did the answer come from?"

"Let's ask the board!"

The pointed responded quickly to their newest question. It spelled D-A-D.

Just then, a knocking came from the wall. The girls jumped.

"What was that?" Carol whispered.

"I don't know."

The slow rap, rap, rap repeated.

"M-maybe it's your father," Carol said, "trying to tell you he's answering your questions."

"You think so?"

Carol raised her eyebrows. "It's real creepy."

"D-dad?" Jenny croaked. "Is that you?"

Rap, rap, rap.

JUMPING!

"If that's you, knock four times."

Rap, rap, rap, rap, giggle.

"What?" Jenny and Carol said it together. Jenny sprang from the bed, ran to the door, flung it open, jumped to the bathroom door.

"Samantha! You twerp! I'll get you for this." Jenny went back into her bedroom and slammed the door. "My ugly sister was knocking on the bathroom wall."

Carol felt back against the bed. "I don't know whether I'm upset or relieved."

"I'm mad," Jenny said. "I hate having a little sister."

"Be thankful you don't have five sisters and brothers, like me."

Jenny sighed. "So where do you think those answers really came from?"

Carol sat up again. "You want to ask the board that one more time? See if it still spells *dad?*"

"Samantha, you twerp!"

Jenny took her position by the board. "Ouija board, tell me the truth. I must know the truth about your answers."

It spelled out D-A-D.

"I need proof," Jenny stated.

Bang! The sound came from her dresser.

"What was that?" Carol asked.

Jenny studied the top of her dresser. Something was different. "Daddy's picture. It fell over!"

Carol squeaked, "Samantha couldn't have done that!"

"No, she couldn't have," Jenny said. "And it's never fallen over by itself before."

The girls looked at each other. "Could it be?" Carol asked.

Jenny looked at the air in front of her dresser. She stretched out a hand into it. The hair on her arm stood up.

"Daddy? Are you there?"

"Daddy? Are you there?"

"This is only a game"

3

The air felt cold. Night had begun to creep in through the window. Jenny shivered. Her hand fell to the Ouija board.

"Do you think my dad's ghost is here?"

Carol gave a short, nervous laugh. "This is only a game, Jenny."

"Let's go downstairs," Jenny said, folding the Ouija board. "I'm not sure we should be doing this. It feels—," Jenny searched for the right word. "Dark."

"That's just the sun going down."

"I guess. But I feel like getting out of this room and being around lots of live people." She stood up and looked at the fallen photo on her dresser.

"Just supposing your father's spirit really is here—and I'm not saying he is—how come you don't want to talk to him?"

"Something doesn't feel right." Jenny hurried to leave the room.

On Sunday evening, Jenny went to the youth group's year-end party at church. She watched the other kids dance and joke around, but she didn't feel like joining in. Her mind kept leaving the room, pulled away by questions about life after death. Who could help her with them? Not her mother. Jenny thought, *Imagine Mom's reaction if I told her I may have talked to Dad!*

Could Alan help Jenny? She watched the youth leader joke around with the other kids. The tall, sandy-haired man was leaning back on his folding metal chair, legs crossed, listening to the Christmas tales of John and Micky. Alan was sort of like a big brother, sort of like a father, but most of all an older and wiser friend. Jenny had often shared her feelings about her father with Alan, and he'd always understood.

When a game came out, Jenny wandered to the kitchen for a paper cup of punch.

Alan

"Is something bothering you tonight, Jenny?" a deep voice asked. Jenny spun around to find Alan standing in the kitchen doorway. "You seem distracted by something."

Jenny shrugged, watching the red juice swirl in her cup.

"The holidays can be depressing when you miss someone," Alan said.

"It's not just that," she answered.

Alan pulled out two chairs from the table and sat on one.

"Do you want to talk about it?" He motioned for her to sit in the empty chair.

"Can a—can someone who's died talk to us from Heaven?"

Alan raised an eyebrow. "What do you mean?"

Jenny took a step closer. "Well, suppose you play with a Ouija board. And suppose you ask it questions you don't know the answers to. And suppose that when it gives the answers, it claims to be someone who's dead."

"Is something bothering you?"

"Hmmm. I think the Bible can help us out with this." He went over to the counter that divided the kitchen from fellowship hall and picked up a Bible. "Did you know the Bible tells us not to fool with Ouija boards?"

"It does? They had Ouija boards back then?"

"No." He thumbed through the pages. "But it's a form of divination—seeking answers from a supernatural source other than God. And the Bible forbids that somewhere in Deuteronomy." He searched more slowly. "Here. See if this helps you." He handed the open Bible to Jenny. "Chapter eighteen, verses fourteen and fifteen."

Jenny read the verses aloud from the New International Version of the Bible. "'The nations you will dispossess listen to those who practice sorcery or divination. But as for you, the Lord your God has not permitted you to do so. The Lord your God will raise up for you a prophet like me from among your own brothers. You must listen to him.'"

"Here. See if this helps"

"Moses wrote that," Alan said. "The prophet he said would come was Jesus Christ. Through Moses, God was telling us that instead of going to Ouija boards or some other form of divination for the answers to our questions, we should go to Jesus."

"But I have asked Jesus — many times — to tell me how my father died. I haven't gotten any answers until now. Couldn't Jesus use a Ouija board to help me?"

Alan frowned. "Would He do that if the Bible says we shouldn't use divination?"

"Maybe Moses meant we shouldn't use divination if we don't believe in God."

Alan paused to think. "When the Ouija board answered your questions, Jenny, where do you think the answers came from?"

"At first I thought they came from my mind."

"But you don't any more?"

"Well—" Jenny put the Bible on the counter. What would Alan think if she told him everything?

"Couldn't Jesus use a Ouija board?"

But if she didn't tell him, who would help her figure things out? "I asked the Ouija board what caused my father's accident. It said a drunken driver did. When I asked it where the answer came from, it spelled out *dad*."

"You think it meant your father?"

Jenny nodded. "I didn't believe it at first, but when I asked for proof, my father's picture fell over, and it's never fallen over by itself before."

Alan sighed. "Jenny, I know you miss him very much, but it's not possible for him to speak to you now."

Jenny turned away so Alan wouldn't see the tears she suddenly had to fight off. "How do you know?" she managed to ask with a steady voice.

"Jesus gave us a parable that explains it. Remember the story in Luke sixteen, verses nineteen to thirty-one, about the rich man who died? He asked Father Abraham to send someone from Heaven to warn his brothers about the punishment that awaited them. Abraham told him

"Jenny, I know you miss him"

no. Abraham said Moses and the other prophets had already warned them."

Jenny shook her head. "But that doesn't apply to my situation. I only wanted God to send my dad to me to help me understand why he died. Certainly God is loving enough and powerful enough to do that."

"Why don't you ask God to show you the truth about the Ouija board?"

Jenny turned to face Alan. "What do you mean?"

"Why don't you ask Him to tell you where the Ouija board's answers come from?"

Alan's suggestion echoed in Jenny's ears when she sprawled out on the floor of Carol's room the next day. She told her friend about their conversation.

Carol grimaced. "He's making too big a deal out of this game. It's not really divination. As long

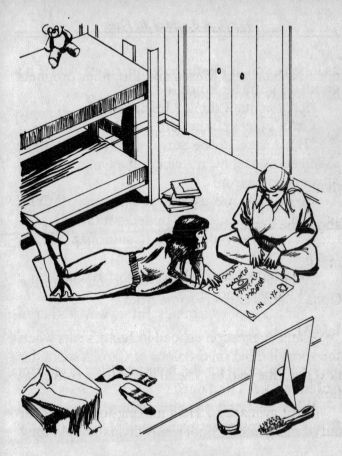

"It's not really divination"

as it helps you, it's gotta be good, right? And if it's good, it's gotta be from God."

"That's what I think," Jenny said.

Carol's face relaxed into a smile.

"But I want to be sure," Jenny added. "I've asked Jesus to show me where the Ouija's board's answers come from."

"Why don't we ask the Ouija board?" Carol headed for her closet and pulled out the game.

"We already did, and it said *dad*," Jenny reminded her.

"So what's the problem?" Carol asked.

"What if it's not my dad?"

"Then it's our own minds. Either way, it's harmless," Carol said.

"I suppose so."

Carol opened up the board and put it in front of Jenny. "Let's find out."

When everything was in position, Jenny looked firmly at the planchette and said, "I want to know

"Let's find out"

the truth." Before she could state the question, the pointer started to move.

The girls watched it go to one letter after another. It moved so quickly, it seemed alive. As they realized what it was spelling, Jenny gasped and covered he mouth with her hands. Even without her fingers on the pointer, it still moved. Until at last it had finished.

Carol's fingers still seemed glued to it. "It can't be true," she said. "Don't believe it, Jenny. It can't be true."

"It can't be true"

"Dad killed another person"

4

All the way home, Jenny's thoughts and emotions swirled in one big mess. The winter wind whipped against her face, but its sting was nothing compared to the pain inside her. Could the Ouija board be right? Or did its horrible message come from her own mind? "Bad drunk," it had spelled out. "Dad killed other person."

It had to be a lie. But where did that answer come from? Her own mind? Did she secretly hate her father? Was the Ouija board giving her a reason to hate him openly?

Or did Carol create that message? The planchette moved when Carol was the only one touching it. But why would her best friend want to hurt her by destroying her love for her dad?

Was it possible the answer came from Jesus? Could that be how He was answering her prayers?

No! The Ouija board couldn't have spoken the truth! Her dad was good and kind and loving. He was not some irresponsible drunk. He was not someone who would kill himself and leave his family fatherless. And he most certainly would never have done anything to kill someone else.

Jenny ran up the driveway to her small split-level, red house. She charged through the door and searched for her mother. Surely she'd be home from work by now. Jenny found her on the old brown living room sofa, her sewing box open beside her. She looked up from the clothes she was mending when Jenny came in. Jenny studied her thin face that was crowned by burly, graying hair.

"Mom," Jenny said, standing across the room with her hands on her hips. "I have to know the truth about Dad."

Mrs. Seker watched her daughter for a long minute, then sighed. "Take off your coat and come sit beside me," she said.

"You'll tell me everything?"

Mrs. Seker looked down at the needle. "I've told you what's important."

"Mom , I have to know the truth"

Jenny dumped her coat on the armchair and sat at the opposite end of the sofa. "But what about the things Uncle Jack and the other relatives say?"

Mrs. Seker shook her head. "Don't let them ruin your memories of your father."

"Are they true?"

Mrs. Seker dropped the mending into her lap. "It's been several years since the accident. Isn't it time you stopped being so obsessed about it and moved on with your life? That's what your father would want."

"But I want to know the truth. Was Dad killed because he was driving drunk?" Jenny watched her mother fidget with the spools of thread in the sewing box, "And did he — did he kill someone else?"

Mrs. Seker gasped and stared at Jenny. "How did you find that out?"

Jenny stood up, her face turning red. "Then it's true?"

"How did you find that out?"

"I don't want you to remember your father that way."

"It's true? He caused the accident? And he took someone else's life?" Jenny backed away.

"Where did you hear that?" Mrs. Seker put aside the mending and moved toward her daughter. "Did Uncle Jack tell you?" The expression on her face turned to anger.

"No, Mom, it wasn't him. It was Carol's Ouija board."

Surprised, Mrs. Seker exclaimed, "Sadie was right. That game is evil!"

"It's not evil. It told me the truth—something *you* wouldn't do."

"Jenny! I was only trying to protect you. It's better that you remember your father for the loving man he was, not for the problem he had."

"Loving! Hah! If he really loved us, he wouldn't have killed himself."

"He had a problem. None of us is perfect."

"Loving! Hah!"

"Why didn't he get help? Didn't he care about what his drinking might do to us?" Tears burned Jenny's eyes. Her mother reached out to touch her arm. Jenny pulled away.

"He loved you very, very much, Jenny. He loved all of us. That's what you have to remember."

"Quit defending him, Mom. If he was drunk all the time, he was evil!"

"He was *not* drunk all the time. And he certainly was not evil. Stop talking this way. If anything's evil, it's that Ouija board. Look what it's done to you," Mrs. Seker said.

"It told me the truth! And I'm glad I finally know it," Jenny yelled. "You've lied to me all these years."

Mrs. Seker stepped toward her daughter, opening her arms, about to reply.

Jenny jumped backward. "I hate Dad for dying that way, and I hate you for lying to me." Jenny spun around and ran for the stairs. "I don't know how the Ouija board knew the truth, but at least it told

"I hate you for lying to me"

me the truth. *That's* not evil!" She stumbled up the stairs and into her bedroom.

Samantha was lying on her bed staring at the ceiling. The book she'd been reading had fallen to the floor.

"You heard?" Jenny asked.

Samantha nodded. "You were shouting loud enough."

"Can you believe what Dad did?"

Samantha just shrugged.

"You don't look very upset about it," Jenny said.

Samantha sat up. "I agree with Mom."

Jenny glared at her sister. "About what?" she snapped.

"The best thing to remember is that he loved us."

"He loved us? You're so naive. Look what he did to us."

"Are you forgetting all the good things he did? I hardly remember them, because I was only six

"I agree with mom"

when he died. But you've told me lots of stories about how wonderful he was."

"I was wrong."

"Do you remember him being drunk around us?" Samantha asked.

"No. He must've hidden it well."

"He never beat us," Samantha said. "He played games with us. He prayed with us at bedtime and read to us. Remember?"

"You just don't want to look at the truth, do you?" Jenny stated.

"*You* don't."

"Hah! You're just siding with Mom to stay on her good side. I don't care what you think, anyway. Nobody around here wants to face the truth, except me, and nobody cares how I feel about it."

Samantha leaned over the side of her bed to pick up her book. "You're not being fair, Jenny."

"Oh, get out of here and leave me alone."

"You can't chase me out. It's my room, too!"

"He prayed with us"

"We would have separate rooms if Dad hadn't killed himself. He forced us to move into this tiny house because it's all Mom can afford. Now get out! I need to be by myself."

Samantha hopped off her bed. "I'll get out, all right, but not because you want me to. I'm leaving because I can't stand being near you."

Jenny shut the door on the heels of her sister. "Twerp," she muttered. Then she looked around the room. Empty. Alone again.

Her eyes fell on the photo of her dad. "Quit smiling!" she said to it. "That smile is hiding evil." She moved closer to her dresser. "How could you be so, so irresponsible? So murderous! And how could I be so wrong about you? I hate you! I'll never forgive you for what you've done!"

She snatched the portrait and threw it across the room. She heard it smash against the wall, but she couldn't see the damage through her hot tears. She flopped down on her bed and cried into her pillow.

"Quit smiling!"

"I wish I had never touched that Ouija board," she sobbed.

Tears of hurt

"I know how you feel"

5

Rap, rap, rap. Someone was knocking on her bedroom door.

"Leave me alone, Sam!" Jenny growled.

"It's your mother, honey. May I please come in?"

Jenny shook her head. Then she looked around the empty room, sat up, wiped the tears from her face and said, "Yes, I guess."

The door opened. Jenny's mother appeared there, her head tilted in concern. "Are you okay?" she asked.

Jenny thought, *Weren't you listening? Of course I'm not okay.* She shrugged.

Her mom sat down on Samantha's bed and faced Jenny, "I know how you feel."

"No, you don't!"

Mrs. Seker sighed. "Yes, I do. Don't forget I was your father's wife. He meant more to me than I can put into words. We had a good marriage. I thought we'd be spending forty or fifty more years together. When the accident happened, I was angry, just like you are now. I missed him and resented him for what he did. I didn't think I could ever forgive him."

Jenny glared at her mother. "Why didn't you stop him from drinking?"

"I tried. I know now I should have tried harder. He never drank as much as some alcoholics do. So I didn't think he had much of a problem. I tried to ignore it because I didn't know what to do about it. I never once imagined it would end up like this." She looked down at her hands and fingered her wedding ring. Her eyes reddened.

"Dad should have been mature enough to get help for his problem himself."

Mrs. Seker spoke softly. "But you need to forgive him, Jenny."

Jenny sprang from her bed. "I can't! I won't! He's messed up our lives, and he's a murderer, too!"

"I tried"

"Jenny," her mother said sternly, "there can be no healing from the hurt unless you forgive him."

Jenny grabbed her pillow and tossed it against the wall. "I don't see how it's possible to forgive him. I don't see how you forgave him so easily."

"It wasn't easy. But I had to, or I'd still be miserable. It's not healthy to dwell on the pain. It's better to remember the good times. Regardless of how your father died, he did love us. He was a good man."

"And he showed his love by driving drunk?" Jenny stomped past her mother.

"What's that on the floor?" Mrs. Seker asked. Jenny glanced at where she was pointing, at the broken photograph beside the desk. The glass was splintered like an evil web across her father's face. She moved away from it.

Mrs. Seker went over and picked it up. "How could you do this? This photo meant so much to you."

"I hate him, Mom."

"How could you do this"

"Don't say that! It's just your hurt talking."

"It's me talking, Mom. You don't understand. All these years I've loved a lie. I hate lies. And I hate Dad for doing what he did."

"Jenny—"

"And you should have told me the truth sooner! No, Mom, you don't understand me at all. I'm going to find someone who does understand me." She fled from the room.

"Where are you going?"

Jenny pounced down the stairs. "To Carol's, I guess."

At Carol's Jenny felt restless being in a home which had a loving father. She suggested that they go to the mall.

"But it's getting close to dinner time," Carol said.

"We'll eat at the Pizza Palace. Will your brother drive us, or will we have to walk?"

Feeling restless

Carol got permission from her mother to eat at the mall. After her big brother, Jimmy, dropped them off, Jenny headed for the music store. Carol had to trot to keep up.

"What's bugging you?" Carol asked the back of Jenny's flying hair. "What happened when you went home earlier?"

Jenny stopped and turned. "The Ouija board was right."

"How do you know?"

"My mother finally told me the truth." She continued her fast walk through the mall.

In the store, the two browsed through the tape racks. The current top hit was playing, but it couldn't drown out Jenny's hurt.

Carol nudged her. "Look who just came in," she whispered. Jenny recognized Phoenix MacLain, an older girl who always wore the latest fashions, from hair to shoes. She'd been held back a grade, so she was in Jenny's classes. Usually she had a flock of

"Look who just come in"

low-achieving friends around her. This time she was alone.

"What is it about her that makes her so popular?" Carol whispered.

Jenny shrugged and mumbled, "Who knows? Maybe it's her looks."

"I wish she'd show me how to do my hair."

"You look fine," Jenny said, louder. "Here's a tape I'd love to have. I can either buy this or buy dinner. Which do you think I should get?"

Carol eyed the tape. "My sister's got that one," she said. "It's really awesome."

"If my dad hadn't killed himself, I'd be getting a big enough allowance to buy dinner *and* this tape."

Another voice said, "Be glad he did kill himself." It was Phoenix. She was standing behind them. It surprised Jenny that this girl from the school's most popular crowd would speak to them. Phoenix shook her permed blonde hair and added, "I wish my father wasn't around any more."

"Be glad he did kill himself"

Jenny gasped. "How can you say that?"

Phoenix grinned. "You don't know what he's like."

"Maybe not, but—"

Phoenix started to walk away.

Carol blurted, "Jenny just found out the truth about how her father died, even though his accident happened six years ago."

"Bummer," Phoenix said without turning.

"My Ouija board told her."

Jenny shot Carol a questioning glance that said, *Why bring that up? You want us to look weird?*

"Oh, really?" Phoenix said, suddenly interested.

Carol nodded energetically. "You have a Ouija board, don't you? I heard you talking about it at school."

Phoenix smiled. "You're telling me that your Ouija board revealed a secret about the death of Jenny's father?"

"Yup," Carol said proudly.

Suddenly interested

Jenny didn't like this conversation. She wanted to get out of the store and find something else to think about.

Phoenix was surveying Jenny. "Did the Ouija say anything else?"

"It said enough," Jenny answered.

"My Ouija board tells me lots of secrets," Phoenix said. "It has supernatural powers, you know."

"Powers?" Carol asked. "Powers to do what?"

Phoenix thumbed her hand across the stacked tapes. "Oh, different things I ask it to do."

"You mean it can do more than answer questions?" Carol's eyes were growing wider by the word.

"Sure, if you know how to use it right."

"Unreal! Hear that, Jenny?"

Jenny frowned. "I thought you said it was just a game."

Carol looked disgusted. "Jen! Get with it."

"My Ouija board tells me secrets"

Carol had never spoken to Jenny like that before. Jenny tried to hide her surprise and mumbled, "It's divination."

"Yeah!" Phoenix said. "Divination. Occult powers. You guys have so much to learn."

"Will you teach us?" Carol asked.

"Sure. But we'll have to do it at your house in case my father comes home."

Jenny felt uneasy about the way this meeting was turning out, If only Carol would notice the warning Jenny was trying to give her with her eyes.

"It's divination"

NEW YEARS EVE

6

Jenny spent the next day, New Year's Eve, in her room. She couldn't be with Carol because the Astreys were visiting relatives. And she didn't feel like hanging around her family. So she tried to convince herself she liked being alone. She buried her father's shattered portrait in the trash by her desk and covered her ears with a headset playing the heavy metal music she had bought at the mall. She felt too gloomy to celebrate the approach of the new year.

When school finally started again, two days later, Jenny told Carol, "This is weird. I'm actually glad to get back to my classes. It's the only thing left in my life that's normal."

At lunch, Carol spotted Phoenix across the room and left Jenny to make plans with her. Upon returning, she said, "Phoenix is coming over to my house after school. She's going to teach us more about the Ouija board's powers."

"I've been thinking about that," Jenny said, toying with the apple her mother had packed. "It seems as if the Ouija board has made my problem worse instead of better."

"How could my Ouija board make things worse?" Carol popped a few corn chips in her mouth. "If you give it another chance, you'll see it can really help you. Phoenix says so."

"Maybe."

By the time the three girls had gathered in Carol's kitchen, Jenny had come to a decision. She would test the Ouija board the way Alan had suggested. While Carol and Phoenix rummaged through the cabinets for a snack, Jenny whispered a prayer: "Dear Jesus, please show me the truth about the Ouija board. If I shouldn't be playing with it, please let me know."

"How about these chocolate cookies?" Carol asked.

"Great," Phoenix said from inside the refrigerator. "You got any diet soda?"

In Carol's kitchen

"Bottom shelf," Carol answered. She took some cookies to Jenny. "Do you think the Ouija board could help Jenny and her problem with her father?"

"Of course," Phoenix said. She popped open an aluminum can and placed it on the table. As she opened the Ouija board, she added, "That's just the beginning of what it can do." She grinned at Jenny. "You want to talk to your father, Jen, and ask him if he really loved you?"

"You think it would be him answering me?"

"Who else would it be?" Phoenix answered. "Carol, get paper and pen to write down what it spells, in case it works fast."

Carol obeyed with growing excitement. Then she seated herself opposite Jenny and poised her pen over the pad. "Let's get started," she said.

Phoenix put her fingers on the planchette and told Jenny to do the same. With her eyes closed, she said, "O powers of the Ouija, come to us and

"Let's get started"

help us. Jenny wishes to speak to her father. O powers of the Ouija, bring him to us."

The pointer began to move. It spelled, *I am here.*

"See that?" Carol whispered, leaning across the table. Jenny frowned back at her.

"If you are Jenny's father," Phoenix continued, "tell us something about yourself."

The Ouija spelled, *Drunk killer.*

That's nothing new, Jenny thought, disgusted. Phoenix eyed Jenny and quickly added, "But you loved your family, didn't you?"

It answered, *Jenny stop praying.*

"What does that mean?" Phoenix asked Jenny, sitting back in her chair. "Are you praying for this not to work?"

Jenny's heart thumped loudly. What would Phoenix think about her now? "I asked Jesus to show me where the Ouija board's answers come from. You have a problem with that?"

"O powers of the Ouija, come to us."

Phoenix shrugged. "Why should I? I don't believe there's a Jesus who can answer you."

"And I don't believe it's my father who's making this pointer move," Jenny said. "He taught me that it's important to pray. He would never tell me to stop praying."

"Maybe not, unless he's discovered in the spiritual plane that prayers don't work," Phoenix said.

"No," Jenny said. "Prayers do work. I'm sure my dad wouldn't tell me to stop praying."

"Then who did?" Carol asked. "It wasn't Phoenix. She didn't even know you *were* praying."

"And it sure wasn't me, so who or what is speaking to us?" Jenny insisted. "I want to find out. Put your fingers back on the planchette, Phoenix. It's my turn to ask a question."

"Be my guest."

With their fingers positioned on the planchette, Jenny said, "Ouija board, tell me the truth. Where do your answers come from?"

"It's my turn to ask a question"

It quickly spelled, *I killed. I kill again. I kill Jenny.*

Jenny jumped out of the chair. "No more! I won't have anything more to do with this. The Ouija is evil. Carol, I wish you'd never gotten me involved in this."

Carol's mouth fell open. She glanced at Phoenix, who sat glumly stroking the planchette. "It is *not* evil!"

"You tell her, Carol," Phoenix goaded.

"I'm your best friend. I would never get you involved in something that's evil."

Jenny wondered why Carol couldn't see the truth. "If it's not evil, why does it want to kill me?"

"Phoenix doesn't think it's evil, and she has a lot more experience with it," Carol insisted. "It's helped you, Phoenix, hasn't it?"

Phoenix smiled and rose from her chair. She leaned close to Jenny. "Yes, the Ouija has helped me. Lots of times. I've never seen it threaten to kill

"No more!"

someone before. It must be *you* that's causing these answers. *You,* Jenny."

"That's right," Carol said, folding her arms across her chest. "The answers came from you. They're from your own mind."

"I'm the only one willing to face the truth," Jenny said, backing away. "I asked Jesus to show me where the answers come from, and *that's* why the Ouija says it wants to kill me. Can't you see that, Carol? Are you blinded by your fascination with —, with —" She waved an arm toward Phoenix. "Phoenix's promise of friendship and supernatural power?"

"You're blinded by your hate for your father," Carol said, unable to meet Jenny's piercing gaze. "I see now we tried doing this too soon after you learned how your father died."

"Aren't you worried about its threat to kill me?"

"The answer came from your mind"

Carol flipped her hair over her shoulders. "How is it going to kill you? Really, Jen. It's just a board."

Jenny realized Carol wouldn't listen. That had never happened in all their years of friendship. "It's evil, I tell you. And I'll find a way to prove it."

"And I'll prove it's good!" Carol shot back.

"Well, I'm not going to hang around watching you try." Jenny reached for her purse and jacket and headed for the front door. It felt wrong leaving her best friend like this. Would Carol try to stop her from leaving?

No. Jenny heard the door close behind her as she walked slowly away.

After she had gone, Carol looked at Phoenix and smiled sheepishly. "She really is an okay person. She's just upset from finding out about her father."

Phoenix sat down and laid the palms of her hands on the Ouija board. "It's her belief in that Jesus fantasy that's messed things up."

Walking away

Carol said nothing, staring off toward the front door.

Phoenix cleared her throat. "So do you want to find out more about the Ouija's powers?" she asked.

"Nah. I'm not in the mood right now." Carol pulled her attention back to her new friend. "But would you help me redo my hair? Your hairstyle looks great on you. No one's ever shown me how to make mine look that good."

Phoenix pushed the planchette to the word *yes.* "Sure. Why not?"

"Help me redo my hair"

Waiting for Phoenix

7

During the second day back to school, Jenny and Carol said little to each other. On the way home, Carol made them wait for Phoenix.

"Why is she hanging around you?" Jenny whispered as they watched her say good-bye to some of her gang. "She's got so many other friends who are more her type."

Carol looked upset. "You jealous or something? Who says I'm not her type?"

"Maybe she only likes you for your interest in the Ouija board."

"What's the difference? She likes me, okay? And you never said anything about my new hair style." Carol fluffed her short-on-top, long-in-back hair.

"It's okay, I guess."

"Just okay?"

"Shh, she's coming."

"So the Jennifer has returned to your side," Phoenix said. "Is she coming to your house to give the Ouija another try?"

Jenny answered, "No, she's just walking with her best friend."

"Oh, I stand corrected." Phoenix bowed with a flourish.

As they made their way through the winding streets, Phoenix related tales of her experiences with the Ouija.

"Once I even used it to help me with my love life!" she said. "I asked it which guy I should go out with. After it gave me the answer, I asked it to go give him the idea to call me. And you know what? He did! That very same night!"

Jenny only half listened. Her best friend was walking beside a girl who, before the holidays, was as likely to care about Carol as a snake would care about a bird it was about to eat. Now here she was, tightly wrapping herself around Carol's life, as if she had no other friends in the world. Why?

"Oh, I stand corrected"

And why did Carol put on such airs to impress her? She was beginning to look like and act like one of Phoenix's gang. This was not the Carol that Jenny had grown up with. Why was she so interested in Phoenix?

Was it because of Phoenix's knowledge of occult powers?

Jenny watched the two of them pull farther and farther ahead. They didn't notice that Jenny was lagging behind. Carol, who used to read every mood Jenny had, now seemed not to care about Jenny's deepening aloneness.

"First I loved my dad," Jenny mumbled. "Then I lost my love and respect for Dad. I've lost my mother's understanding. I've lost a sister to the enemy's side. And now I'm losing Carol!" Jenny couldn't — she wouldn't — believe it.

Jenny split toward her own house. Carol waved a quick good-bye without pausing in her conversation with Phoenix.

"Now I'm losing control"

A little later, as Jenny tried to do her homework, she wondered what Carol and Phoenix were doing right then. It used to be Jenny that Carol got together with after school. Was Jenny losing her best friend to that intruder? Friends for life, Jenny and Carol had promised. So why didn't Carol care about Jenny's feelings any more?

She was afraid she knew the answer to that. Phoenix and the powers of the Ouija board were changing Carol.

Jenny opened a drawer and pulled out a photo album. She flipped to a picture of Jenny and Carol fooling around on a kiddie jungle gym.

"Carol," she said, "I'm not going to lose you. I'm not going to let Phoenix — or your stupid Ouija board — ruin our friendship. That's a promise."

When Carol and Phoenix entered the Astrey house, Phoenix rejected the idea of doing homework together. "Let's get out the Ouija board instead," she said.

Friends for life

"Will you teach me how to use its supernatural powers?" Carol asked after she had chased a sister from her room.

Phoenix carefully spread the Ouija on the floor and examined the planchette. "The power is yours if you believe in it."

"I do believe!"

"Then let's get started."

Carol took her position by the board. *If only Jenny were here,* she thought. They had always shared in everything before. What a pity Jenny was missing this. What had gotten into her, anyway?

"O, powers of the Ouija, come to us," Phoenix intoned after Carol placed her fingers ever-so-lightly on the planchette. "I have someone new to offer you," Phoenix continued. "Come accept her into the realm of your powers. Tell us, do you approve of her?"

The planchette immediately moved to the word *yes.*

"I have someone new to offer you"

Phoenix whispered to Carol with a grin, "I knew you were psychically in tune. Now ask the Ouija something."

Carol cleared her throat, trying to hold back her nervous excitement. "I want something I can use as proof to Jenny that the Ouija's powers are good. Is there some information about her father, about how he loved her, that would help her get through this rough time she's having?"

Phoenix rolled her eyes to show she was getting tired of Jenny, but she said, "O powers of the Ouija, bring Jenny Seker's father to us that we might ask him to help us."

The pointed began to move. *I am here,* it spelled.

Carol felt a cold wave roll past her. It seemed as if an unseen presence had joined them. "If you are Jenny's father," she said, "tell us something about your love for Jenny that would make her feel better about you."

Reggie gone but always with her.

"Asking the Ouija"

"Do you understand that?" Phoenix asked Carol.

Carol shook her head. "I never heard of a Reggie. Her father's name was William. I'll ask Jenny if she knows what it means, then I'll tell you what she says."

"Now it's my turn to help Jenny," Phoenix said, returning the planchette to the center of the board. "Where do the Ouija's powers come from?"

It answered, *Spirit world.*

"That's what I thought," Phoenix said with a grin. "Is there something you'd like the Ouija to help *you* with, Carol?"

Carol thought for a minute. The Ouija couldn't possibly give her what she wanted most — a bedroom of her own. And now that she had one of the most popular girls in school as a friend, being well-liked was already being taken care of. She could ask the Ouija to make Mark Talbot call her. Or she could ask it to help Jenny become friends with Phoenix and the Ouija board.

Thinking up a question

"Well?" Phoenix said, getting impatient.

The phone rang twice. Before Carol could answer Phoenix, a sister's voice called her to pick up the phone.

It was Jenny on the other end. She asked, "Is Phoenix still there?"

"You'll never guess what the Ouija board told us!" Carol said.

"I don't think I want to know."

"Does the name *Reggie* mean anything to you?"

"No."

"Well, when I asked the Ouija for proof that your father loved you, it said, 'Reggie gone but always with her.'"

Jenny said nothing.

"Does that mean anything?" Carol asked.

"I almost forgot," Jenny said slowly. "Reggie was a yellow parakeet my dad bought for me when I was five. He only lived a few months, but I really loved that bird. Daddy came home from work early the day Reggie died. He hugged me for a long time.

126

"Does the name Reggie mean anything"

And he kept telling me that even though Reggie was gone, he would always be with me in spirit."

"Wow! Then it must really have been your dad who spoke to us through the Ouija board."

"No, I don't think so," Jenny replied. "I still think the Ouija board is evil."

Carol shifted her feet and glanced toward her bedroom. "How can you say that after it reminded you of a good memory of your father?"

"Look what it's doing to our friendship," Jenny said.

"What *it's* doing?" Carol shouted. "No, it's *you*, Jenny. You don't care about what's important to me any more. If you did, you'd explore the powers of the Ouija board with me and you'd approve of my friendship with Phoenix."

She slammed down the phone receiver.

Breaking connection

"This is all your fault, dad"

8

Jenny stared at the kitchen phone. She thought, *Carol wouldn't hang up on me. Not Carol. I'm sure she's dialing back right now. I'm sure that phone's going to ring any second.*

But the phone remained silent.

Jenny sat down at the table and laid her arms on its cold surface. A frightening sense of aloneness welled up through her like a deep, drowning sea.

"Carol," Jenny screamed. The sound echoed off the walls. "What's happened to our friendship?" She laid her head on her arms. "This is all your fault, Dad."

Jenny scraped her chair across the floor tiles as she pushed away from the table. "Dear Jesus, I'm so alone. I know You're here, but I can't feel Your presence any more. Won't You please bring this loneliness to an end? I don't know how to get Carol back. I don't know how to undo what Phoenix and the Ouija board have done."

Who could she call? Who would help her? Alan came to mind. Yes, he understood her! He understood about Ouija boards, too. She looked up his number in the address book and prayed he would be home. He was probably at work, and she'd be embarrassed about calling, but at least it gave her something to try.

His deep voice answered after a few rings.

"You're home!" she blurted.

"I took the day off to fix my wife's car. What can I do for you?"

Jenny prayed silently, *Thank You, Jesus!* She told Alan, "You were right about the Ouija board, and now it's stealing my best friend from me. I don't know what to do."

"Let's talk about it at church. Do you have a way to get there?"

"No. My mom's at work."

"Then I'll pick you up."

Alan answering Jenny's call

As they entered the sanctuary together and sat down on the front pew, Jenny sensed a peacefulness she hadn't felt at home. In a quiet tone, she finished describing her problem to Alan. "I can't believe Carol's treating me like this. Sometimes I think it's Phoenix's fault, but I can't figure out why Phoenix is interested in Carol. The only thing they have in common is the Ouija board."

"Would you say the Ouija board has a power over Carol?" Alan asked.

Jenny frowned. "Phoenix keeps saying it has powers."

"And where do its powers come from?"

"At first I thought from our minds. But some of its answers have been supernatural."

"There are only two sources of supernatural power," Alan said. "One is God, but we know the Ouija board's answers didn't come from Him, since He tells us not to use divination. And we know God didn't send your father or any other spirits of

Meeting in Church

people, since He doesn't allow the dead to speak to the living. So what's left?"

Jenny didn't know.

Alan answered, "What evil supernatural forces are there except demons?"

Jenny gasped. "I didn't know demons were real."

"Jesus did. He spoke to them and cast them out of people."

A horrifying thought hit Jenny. "You don't think Carol's possessed, do you?"

"Not at all," Alan assured her. "But whenever we open ourselves to the demons of the occult, we open ourselves to their influence. You see, Jenny, every occult power comes from Satan. He uses the occult to keep people from knowing the love of Jesus and His greater supernatural power. But he hides that fact from people like a dark secret."

"So how do I convince Carol she's playing with demons?" Jenny asked. "Should I, with Jesus' help, ask the Ouija board to tell Carol the truth?"

"I didn't know demons are real"

"No," Alan said. "Stay away from it. The evil spirit behind it hates you because you belong to Jesus. Don't give it a chance to do something to you."

"You mean it could kill me, the way it said?" Jenny asked, her eyes widening with fear.

"No, Jesus is protecting you. But it could look for some way to destroy your relationship with God. Don't give it that opportunity."

Jenny nodded. "So how do I get Carol away from it?"

Alan stroked his face thoughtfully. "The power of Jesus is stronger than the power of the Ouija. When Jesus died on the cross for our sins and then conquered death on Easter morning, He conquered all of Satan's powers."

Jenny looked up at the large cross hanging on the wall behind the altar. Light from the setting sun was passing through a stained-glass window, illuminating the cross with a rainbow of colors. "And

"The power of Jesus is stronger"

Jesus can conquer the demon that Carol and Phoenix are playing with?"

"Definitely," Alan said, "if we ask God to bless Carol's occult activities."

"Bless them?" Jenny gave Alan a startled glance. "Why would God bless something that's evil?"

"For the same reason Jesus told us to pray for our enemies. The cure for evil is goodness. In first Peter three, verse nine, the Bible says that instead of returning evil for evil, we should give a blessing. What do you think happens when God blesses something?"

Jenny let the possibilities roll through her mind. "He makes it holy. So if I ask Him to bless Carol's Ouija board, He'd make it holy?"

"Not exactly." Alan shifted his long legs. "The powers behind the occult can never be made holy, since they're demonic. But if we ask God to bless Carol's Ouija board the next time she plays with it,

"Why would God bless something evil?"

He will surround it with His holiness. Any demons connected to it will flee."

"Then let's pray now!" Jenny insisted.

Alan took Jenny's hands and bowed his head. "Holy Father in heaven, in the name of Your Son Jesus Christ, we ask You to bless Carol's Ouija board when Carol and Phoenix use it. We ask You to fill the room with Your holy presence so that no demons can remain near Carol and Phoenix. We thank You for Your help, dear God."

"Why isn't it moving?" Carol asked.

Phoenix swore.

"It's like the Ouija's power suddenly left," Carol said.

"It did." Phoenix closed her eyes again. "Come back, o great powers of the Ouija!"

They waited. The planchette remained motionless.

Phoenix jumped up. "It's Jenny's doing."

"What? How could that be?"

Power praying

"I don't know how she's doing it, but I can feel it," Phoenix said. "There's a different presence here. I don't like it." Phoenix grabbed her coat from the bed and backed toward the door.

"Wait!" Carol pleaded. "Why don't we try to communicate with that presence?"

"No. I have to go." Phoenix scooted down the stairs.

Carol ran after. "Don't leave yet, Phoenix! Why can't we call the Ouija's powers back?"

Phoenix threw on her jacket. "Jenny's done something to block it. Find out what she's doing. Then make her stop."

"Before you go home," Alan said to Jenny, "I think there's something else you need to do."

"Sure. What?"

"Forgive your father."

"How do you know he did something that needs forgiveness?" she replied. She didn't remember telling him about that part of her problem.

"Jenny's done something"

Alan looked her squarely in the eyes. "I don't know what he did or what you think he did, but when we were praying, I sensed God saying you need to forgive him."

Jenny jumped from the pew. "My mother told you, didn't she? She doesn't understand why I can never forgive him. So she asked you to talk to me about it. Didn't she?"

"No, she didn't."

"Cover for her, if you like, but what my father did was unforgivable." She stalked down the darkening aisle.

"What my father did was unforgivable"

"How did you do it?"

9

Not long after Jenny returned home from church, Carol knocked on the Sekers' door. One of Phoenix's hoop earrings dangled beneath Carol's new hair style. She smiled, but with a glint of determination that sent chills through Jenny.

"Your new best friend isn't with you?" Jenny asked as she let Carol in.

"How did you do it?" Carol demanded.

"Do what?"

"Block the Ouija's power. We know you did something."

"You mean the Ouija board didn't work?" Jenny asked, beaming.

"What did you do to stop it?" Carol said more loudly.

Wow! The prayers really worked, Jenny thought. She stood between Carol and the door, with her arms crossed, and said, "How do you know I did something?"

"Phoenix figured it out," Carol snarled. "Why would you do such a thing? I thought you were my friend."

Jenny raised her eyebrows. "I don't think Phoenix is the right kind of friend for you."

"So you're trying to break us up by blocking the Ouija's power?" Carol's face reddened.

Jenny glowered back. "That's *not* why I blocked its powers. But if Phoenix stops hanging around you because the Ouija board doesn't work, so much the better. Phoenix has ruined our friendship."

"No, *you* ruined our friendship." Carol jabbed her in the shoulder with a finger. "You used to enjoy the same things I do. You used to want me to be happy."

"I do want you to be happy," Jenny said. "But the Ouija board is *not* going to make you happy. It's evil. I've been trying to tell you that, but you won't listen. You used to listen to me."

"You're narrow-minded." Carol poked Jenny again. "It is not evil."

"You're narrow-minded"

"If it's not evil, then why did Jesus stop it from working?"

"What does Jesus have to do with it?" Carol said, disgusted. "Phoenix is right: You *are* overly religious."

Jenny put her hands on her hips. "I asked Jesus to be with you when you played with the Ouija. And since demons flee from Jesus, they weren't around to make your Ouija board work."

"Demons!" Carol shrieked. "What do you think I am? A devil worshiper? All I'm doing is playing with a Ouija board. Demons! Hah! I don't know you anymore, Jenny. You never used to talk this way. Phoenix said you're ruining things, and she's right. If that's the kind of friend you want to be, we're through." Carol shoved Jenny aside, plowed through the doorway, and slammed the door shut.

Jenny balled her hands into fists as she stared at the closed door. "Well, Carol," she huffed, "if

"We're through"

that's the kind of friend *you* want to be, I don't *want* you to be my friend!"

Jenny's determination to stay angry at Carol made her decide to avoid the next youth meeting. The planned topic was "Forgiving Even When It Hurts."

"I think you should go," Jenny's mother told her during lunch.

"I just don't feel like it, okay?" Jenny retorted.

Samantha said, "I'd go, if I were old enough."

Jenny grimaced at her. "You two are ganging up on me again. Why can't I do what I want to do?"

"Dear," Mrs. Seker said, "I'm only thinking of how it could help you."

"You're still on my case about Dad," Jenny said. "Forgiving him won't change the past or the present."

"But it would help you with Carol," Mrs. Seker said.

"You two are ganging up on me"

Carol and Phoenix set up the Ouija board in Carol's darkened bedroom.

"Are you sure Jenny doesn't know we're doing this right now?" Phoenix asked.

"She doesn't know anything I'm doing anymore," Carol said unhappily.

"We'll soon find out if she's been praying again," Phoenix said.

Carol hesitated before putting her fingers on the planchette. "If prayers can stop the Ouija's power, are we so sure the Ouija is good?"

Phoenix laughed. "We're just having some fun. If Jenny was really a good friend, why would she try to stop you from having fun?"

Carol shrugged.

Phoenix picked up the planchette and waved it in front of Carol. "If we're going to tap into more of the Ouija's powers, we can't have Jenny interfering. Fortunately, the Ouija can help us stop her. Are you ready?"

"I guess."

"Are you ready?"

With fingers and planchette in position, Phoenix closed her eyes and called on the Ouija's power. "O great Ouija, there is an obstacle to our reaching higher levels of psychic awareness. Her name is Jenny Seker. Can you stop her from interfering?"

The pointer moved to *yes*.

The car bounced as Jenny sat in the backseat while her mother drove her to the youth meeting. Outside the window, the sky was dark, starless. A sense of something going wrong crept into Jenny. She wished she had stayed home. The closer they got to the church, the stronger her wish grew. She thought of Samantha back home and wanted to be with her.

Jenny tried to relieve tension by stretching her legs across the seat. She had to take her seat belt off to feel comfortable. But even that position didn't relax her.

Driving to youth meeting

She watched her mother steer through the traffic. She looked so alone, a single mother whose husband could still be alive, if only — And yet, she had forgiven him. How? Could Jenny?

The headlights of a car coming down a side street glared brightly and made Jenny squint. As they continued to grow brighter, Jenny realized the car was coming right at them, not stopping. Jenny screamed, tires squealed, metal crunched, the car jerked sideways, and the lights went black.

The next lights Jenny saw were square, blurred lights, one rushing into another. The car was still moving. No, it was not the car. Jenny was on a stretcher, being wheeled down a bright hallway. A bag of clear liquid hovered above her, held by the hand of a man running beside her. Voices, many voices, hung around her.

And then she felt the pain. It seemed as if the inside of her left leg was on fire! She tried to cry out, but the light returned to darkness.

"Jenny, Jenny," a woman's voice called.

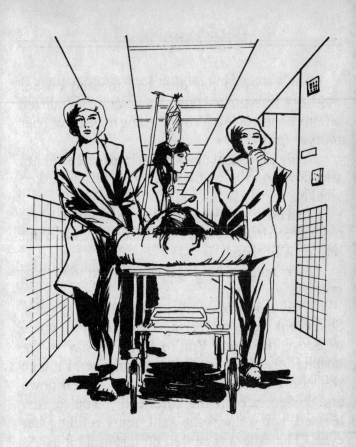

"JENNY, JENNY!"

Jenny opened her eyes and focused on her mother's tear-soaked face. A few scratches marred an expression of joy. "You're going to be okay," her mother said.

Jenny tried to sit up, but dizziness forced her to stay down on the bed. "Where am I?" she asked weakly.

"In a hospital. We were in a car accident, hit by a drunken driver. You're a little banged up. Your left leg is broken."

Jenny realized her leg no longer felt like it was burning.

"They gave you medicine for the pain," Mrs. Seker said. "You're wearing a cast from your ankle to above the knee. You're going to stay in the hospital overnight for observation. Then I'll take you home tomorrow." Her mother leaned down and kissed her on the forehead. "You're very blessed, you know," she said, tears refilling her eyes. "The other car veered off just as it hit us. As if something pushed it away. I'd hate to think of

"You're very blessed"

what would have happened if it had hit us full force. We have much to thank God for."

"Carol," Jenny said.

"Huh?"

"Tell Carol what happened to me."

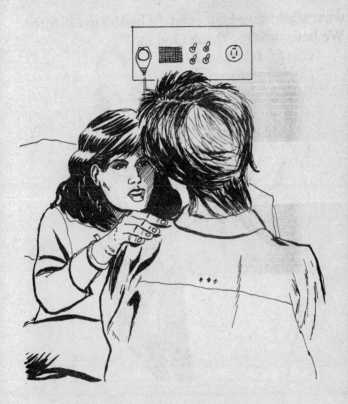

"Tell Carol what happened to me"

"You look as if you've seen a ghost"

10

Carol's face turned white. She hung up the phone slowly, unable to move, her thoughts racing. Phoenix stepped into the lighted hallway from the semi-darkness of Carol's room. Seeing Carol's expression, she laughed.

"You look like you've seen a ghost!" she said.

"Jenny's been in an accident." Carol glared at Phoenix. "She's in the hospital! They were on their way to church when they were hit by another car. Her leg's busted up. She could have been killed!"

Phoenix shrugged. "That'll stop her from meddling with our Ouija for a while."

Carol gasped. "You sound as if you're happy she's hurt!"

Phoenix chewed her gum loudly for a minute before she replied. "Of course I'm not happy about it."

"Don't you feel at all guilty that maybe we caused the accident?" Carol asked.

Phoenix snickered. "Really, Carol. How could we be responsible? We were here when it happened."

"Yeah, we were here playing with that Ouija board. You were telling it to do something to stop Jenny from interfering." Her voice rose. "She could have been killed!"

Phoenix shushed her and yanked her back into the bedroom. "We had nothing to do with the accident," she said in a hushed tone. "If it happened because of the Ouija's powers—and I think that would prove just how awesome the Ouija's powers are—it still wouldn't be our fault. We told the Ouija our problem. *It* decided what to do about it. *It* did the deed, not us. *It* knows better than we do how to solve our problems."

Carol's jaw dropped open. "I don't believe I'm hearing this! So what if we didn't tell it to cause an accident? We told it to stop her. It's our fault. And if she'd gotten killed—" Her chin quivered as she fought back tears. She leaned on her dresser to

"Really, Carol"

keep her weakening knees from collapsing. She accidentally knocked over a glass owl that Jenny had given her. *Thank goodness this didn't break,* she thought as she picked it up.

Phoenix grabbed Carol by the shoulders. "Did you want the Ouija to kill Jenny?"

"Of course not!"

"And I didn't, either. And I'm sure neither of us wanted her to get her leg broken. So we're not to blame. It's not our fault."

Carol squirmed free from Phoenix's grasp and turned on all the room lights. "So you're saying it's only the Ouija's fault?"

"You're catching on, now." Phoenix smiled.

"What *is* the Ouija, that it can do this?"

Phoenix shrugged. "A higher spiritual force."

"A demon?"

Phoenix doubled over with forced laughter. "You heard that from Jenny, didn't you?"

Carol blushed. "How do you know it's not evil?"

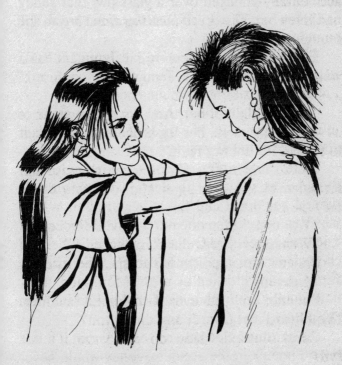

"Did you want the Ouija to kill Jenny?"

"How could an evil spirit do good, as this Ouija has done?"

"How could a spirit that's *not* evil try to kill someone?"

"Who says it even tried to kill Jenny? It could have been coincidence. You're just confused," Phoenix said, sitting down on a bed.

"You're right about that. Leave me alone to think." She plucked Phoenix's jacket from a chair and tossed it to the girl.

Later that night, Carol wrestled with her thoughts as she tried to sleep. Guilt and doubt pinned her down and threw her around. Whose face was that on the enemy? Jenny's? Phoenix's? Too dark to see. The Ouija's? It laughed at her and choked her with its poisonous breath. Then she saw Jenny getting crushed by a car. More laughter—now coming from Phoenix. Carol bolted up from her pillow.

As her mind cleared, she realized that if it had been Phoenix in the accident, Jenny would never

Carol bolting up from her pillow

have laughed about it. Even though Jenny didn't like Phoenix, she would have cared. Jenny was the better friend. Why hadn't she seen that before?

After school the next day, Carol visited Jenny, who was now home, lying on the sofa under blankets. Her leg was in a large cast and propped up by pillows. A coffee table in arm's reach was cluttered with books, tissues, a radio, a soda can and other "necessities." Though her face was swollen with bruises, Jenny smiled.

"I'm glad you came," she said.

"Are you okay?" Carol asked, taking a nervous step closer.

"It hurts some. And this sofa is fast becoming uncomfortable. But I'm all right."

"I—I think I know how it happened," Carol said feebly.

"A drunken driver," Jenny said with disgust.

"No, I mean *why*—" Carol wanted to gain Jenny's trust again by telling her everything. But

Jenny at home

would telling her help or make things worse? She wanted Jenny to know how very sorry she was for asking the Ouija to do something to her. But could she find the right words?

"*Why* it happened?" Jenny asked, snarling. "People drive drunk because they don't care about anyone else. Like my father. But I'm glad it happened."

Carol's face showed the surprise she felt.

Jenny continued. "Yup, I'm actually glad. Want to know why? Because it reminded me of the evil thing my father did. You wouldn't believe where I was going when the accident happened. To a meeting on forgiveness! Hah! I was actually thinking I might forgive my father. But that drunken driver who did this to me reminded me of just how evil drunken driving is. It reminded me that I should never forgive my father."

Carol didn't know how to respond.

"Quit standing there with your mouth open," Jenny said, "and tell me why you came."

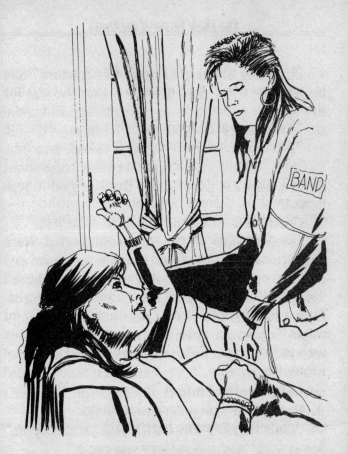

"I'm glad it happened"

"I wanted to tell you I'm—" Carol couldn't get the next word out. A giant lump of fear blocked her throat.

"You're what?" Jenny said, her tone softening.

"Ahh, I'm glad you weren't hurt worse."

"Oh." Jenny looked disappointed. "Well, I guess I had an angel protecting me. My mom says it seemed as if some invisible force pushed the other car aside so it wouldn't hit us full force."

"Do you think an evil spirit could have caused the accident?" Carol asked quietly.

"Never thought about that." Jenny paused. "Maybe. But we can't put the blame on evil spirits. That other driver chose to get drunk, and then he chose to drive. Just like you can't blame evil spirits for what my father did. It was his choice. That's why I can't forgive him."

Carol shuffled a foot and stared at the floor. After an awkward silence, Jenny said, "Is there anything else you came here for?"

Fear blocked her throat

Carol wanted to answer yes. She wanted to say something that would restore their friendship. But she was afraid Jenny wouldn't forgive her if she knew what Carol knew about the accident.

"Carol," Jenny said.

"Huh?"

"I *am* glad you came."

Their eyes met, and they quickly looked elsewhere. It was a moment of hope slipping through the cracks of fear and unforgiveness.

"I wish we could be friends again," Carol blurted before she could chicken out.

Jenny's face turned quickly to a smile. Just as quickly, it dissolved. "What about Phoenix?" she asked. "You told me you don't want me interfering in your friendship with her."

Carol face her face get hot. "You didn't have to bring her into this."

"She's part of the problem, whether I bring her into this or not," Jenny replied.

"I'm glad you came"

"Why can't you trust me?" Carol asked. "You don't think I can figure out who's a good friend and who's not!"

"You've become a different person!" Jenny shouted back.

Carol glared at her ex-friend. She felt smothered by Jenny's unforgiveness. To breathe again, she'd have to get out of there. She turned and fled.

Leaving

Running home

11

Carol did not feel the chill of the winter day as she ran home. Heated by her anger and hurt, she raced her memory through the events that had left her without a best friend.

Each memory filled her with the same emotion: She hated herself for not finding a way to make up with Jenny; she hated Jenny for hating Phoenix; she hated Phoenix for knowing so much about Ouija boards.

Oh, how she longed for everything to be the way it was before she got that Ouija board.

At home she headed straight for her room. She pulled the Ouija board from the closed shelf and held it, frozen by a moment of confusion. Was this the cause of her problems? She still didn't believe it had a demon, but if only she had never gotten this so-called game. Then she and Jenny would still be friends.

Angrily, she tore open the box and grabbed the board and ripped it apart at its middle seam. Then she broke it over the back of the chair. When she had demolished it into several pieces, she threw the planchette on the floor and stomped on it. Then she surveyed the mess.

The air seemed heavy. Though sunlight streamed through the window, darkness seemed to hover around her. Carol shivered. She sank to the lower bunk that was her bed. The upper bunk's shadow swallowed her up. She shivered again. Was one of her sisters in here? Carol sensed someone's eyes watching her. But she was alone.

She decided to open her curtains wider. A sunbeam touched her dresser and caught the gold paint on one of her glass knickknacks. It was an angel Jenny had given her a long time ago.

"Oh, Jenny," Carol moaned. She went to the dresser and reached for the angel, but when she picked it up, it cracked in her hand. She almost cut herself on its sharp edges. How could that have

Breaking the Ouija board

happened? Had one of her sisters dropped it and put it back, pretending nothing had broken? That sounded like something Darlene would do.

"I'll strangle her," Carol said. "This was one of my favorite presents from Jenny." She picked up the owl. It, too, shattered in her hand.

"I don't believe this! Yesterday it was fine." She touched a glass flower. Broken. A teddy bear. Broken. A kitten. Broken. All of them, every one that Jenny had given her, broken. But *only* those that Jenny had given her.

"This is too weird," Carol said. Who was watching her? She looked around, expecting to find one of her sisters. Now her bed was unmade! She had just sat on it, and she was sure it had been covered by the blankets. Now the blankets were tossed into a lump at the bottom.

"All right, Darlene," Carol said, trying to steady her voice. "Come out from hiding. I know you messed up my bed." Carol searched under the beds and in the closet. No Darlene.

Broken

With a growing, eerie feeling, she said, "I don't like this." She looked at the pieces of the Ouija board on the floor and felt goose bumps rise. "I must get rid of that." She scooped up the pieces, carried them downstairs to the kitchen, and dumped them into the trash.

"Carol!" her mother called from upstairs.

"What, Mom?" Carol called back as she passed through the dining room to get nearer.

"Get up here right now and clean up this mess. You know the rules."

"What mess?" Carol stood at the bottom of the stairs.

"You know what I'm talking about, young lady. Get up here now."

"I thought I picked up all the Ouija board pieces," Carol mumbled to herself. At the top of the stairs, she found her mother waiting for her. As Carol moved closer, she spotted her clothes lying all over her bedroom floor. Her dresser drawers were open and empty.

Disaster

"I didn't do that," Carol said. "I was just up here and it wasn't like that. Honest, Mom. It must have been Darlene or Beth playing tricks on me."

Mrs. Astrey spoke sternly. "Your sisters are at their friends' houses."

"Then who—?" Carol shivered again. She suddenly did not want to go into that room, but her mother's face told her she had better clean up that mess *now*. Carol hurried to put the clothes away, concentrating on the job rather than on how the mess got there. Afterward, she grabbed the phone in the hallway and called Phoenix.

"Why did you smash your Ouija board?" Phoenix wanted to know.

"I was really mad about losing Jenny's friendship," Carol answered.

"Why take it out on the Ouija?"

"Everything started going bad after I got that thing," Carol said.

"Everything? What about *our* friendship?" Phoenix made a poor imitation of feeling hurt.

192

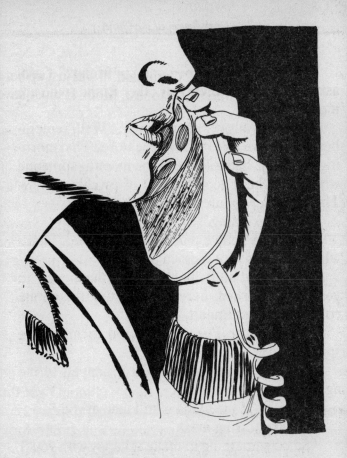

"What about our friendship?"

"Just why *did* you become my friend?" Carol asked. "You have plenty of other friends who are more your type."

Phoenix's answer came slowly. "Well, remember that day we met in the music store? That morning, my Ouija had told me I'd be meeting someone who would be a good student of psychic powers. The Ouija set up our friendship."

"You're kidding."

"And now you've made the Ouija mad. That's why your things got messed up."

"Has weird stuff like that ever happened to you?" Carol asked, nervously twisting the phone cord around her fingers.

"No, because I've never dared to make the spirits mad."

Carol eyed her room. "Will it happen to me again?"

"It might. If the Ouija is still mad at you."

"You're scaring me."

"So do something to make it happy with you."

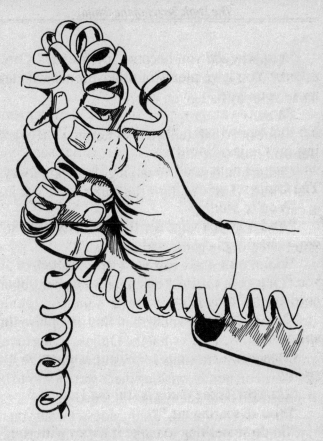

"You're scaring me"

"Like what?"

"Well, didn't you say it broke just the knick-knacks Jenny had given you?"

"Yes."

"Doesn't that tell you something? It wants Jenny out of your life."

"I don't believe we're talking about it this way," Carol said. "I used to think the Ouija board was just a game."

"There's an Ouija spirit for everyone who's interested in the game," Phoenix said.

"I don't want any spirits," Carol replied.

"Of course you do. The Ouija is a higher, supernatural intelligence who can help you. Jenny doesn't want you to know that. So she's poisoning your thoughts. That's what the Ouija is trying to tell you. That's why it wants Jenny out of your life."

Carol bit her lip, wishing there were a way to be friends with both Jenny and Phoenix.

Phoenix continued. "Jenny doesn't want you to develop our psychic powers. The Ouija does, be-

"The Ouija wants Jenny out of your life"

cause it knows these powers will make your life better."

Carol was really getting confused. Jenny had been a great friend, better than Phoenix. But Phoenix's words sounded true. "Tell me how to make the Ouija spirit leave me alone," she said.

"You don't want it to leave you alone," Phoenix responded. "It can teach you many things and give you powers beyond your dreams. You just want it to not be angry at you. You have to get Jenny out of your life. She's your block to reaching greater powers."

"I don't want her out of my life. If the Ouija is so powerful, why won't it help me get her back?"

"Haven't you been listening? She's no good for you."

"She was good for me before I started fooling with the Ouija board."

"But your life can get so much better now."

"It's been getting worse!" Carol exclaimed.

"How can I make the Ouija leave me alone?"

"Only because Jenny's still in your life," Phoenix insisted.

"Actually, she's not. I tried to make up with her, but it didn't work. The Ouija wrecked my stuff even though Jenny's already out of my life."

"But you still want to be friends with her," Phoenix said. "That's what the Ouija doesn't like."

"Why should I do what the Ouija wants?" Carol wanted to know. "Why can't I make my own decisions about who I have for friends?"

"Because it knows what's best for you."

"It's trying to control my life," Carol said. "I'm going to make up my own mind about who's a good friend and who's not."

Phoenix was silent for a moment. Then she said, "Suit yourself. I tried to help you. It's up to you whether or not the Ouija stays angry at you. Don't blame me for what it does next."

"Don't blame me for what happens next"

"Take me to Carol!"

12

Carol stared at the door to her room and steadied herself by holding onto a hallway wall.

"Oh, Jenny," she groaned. "Help me!" Should she call her? Would Jenny be willing to help? Would Jenny know how to get rid of the Ouija spirit? "God, help me!" she cried.

"Take me to Carol's house," Jenny told her mother.

"The doctor says you must rest with your leg up," Mrs. Seker said, checking the pillows under the cast.

"I've got to talk to Carol". Jenny tried to lift her broken leg.

"Why don't you call her?"

"She might hang up on me," Jenny said. She eased her foot onto the floor. "Will you take me there? Please?"

Mrs. Seker shook her head. "I know how important this is, but—"

"I've had nothing to do but sit here all afternoon, thinking of how I blew it with Carol today. I have to straighten things out before it's too late." Jenny reached for her crutches.

Mrs. Seker studied her daughter's determination.

"Please, Mom! I've been praying about this. I believe this is what God wants me to do."

"How long will it take?"

"Fifteen minutes, tops. I promise."

When Jenny and her mother arrived at the Astrey home, Carol greeted them with a look of surprise. While Mrs. Seker joined Mrs. Astrey in the kitchen, Carol helped Jenny into a soft living room chair.

"What are you doing here?" Carol asked as she stood awkwardly nearby.

"I want to apologize for earlier today," Jenny said.

"SURPRISE!"

"I'm sorry, too," Carol said.

"And I also want to tell you something that's very important. I'm not sure how to say it." She rubbed her cast, feeling a pain worse than her leg's.

"But the Ouija board has gotten between us," Carol finished.

"Right!"

"It's evil."

"Right!" Jenny wanted to jump up and hug Carol. "But how did you figure that out?"

"Anything that has the power to break stuff when no one's in the room and tries to break up a good friendship, too, has to be evil."

"What do you mean, 'break stuff?'"

Carol told her about the spooky things that had been happening. Jenny's eyes grew wider as she listened.

"But that's not all that convinced me it's evil," Carol said, happy that Jenny was showing concern. "The Ouija was the cause of your accident."

"Huh?" Jenny stiffened.

"The Ouija caused your accident"

"Since you wanted to stop the Ouija board's powers, Phoenix and I asked the Ouija to stop you."

"You did what?" Jenny gasped.

"I didn't want it to hurt you," Carol added quickly. "I had no idea it would try to stop you by almost getting you killed."

"I don't believe you did that!" Jenny felt trapped in her cast. She wanted to jump up. "A couple of weeks ago, you were my best friend, and now you're trying to kill me?"

"I tried to tell you I'm sorry," Carol said, feeling hurt by Jenny's reaction. "But I was afraid it would ruin any chances of us making up, because of what you said about your dad."

"What about my dad?" Jenny's eyes narrowed.

"You won't forgive him. I figured you'd never forgive me, either."

"How could you do this to me? How could you —you who used to be my best friend —you sent a demon to stop me from trying to help you!" Jenny struggled to lift herself off the chair.

"I didn't want to hurt you"

"I didn't know it was evil," Carol said.

"I *tried* to warn you," Jenny shot back. "Mom! I want to go." She struggled to stand on the cast and fell back into the chair. "You did this to me. You, who used to be my best friend."

Mrs. Seker entered the room. "Is everything all right?" she asked.

"Take me home *now*," Jenny said.

Carol watched Mrs. Seker help Jenny hobble away on the crutches. As their car pulled out of the driveway, Carol grabbed her jacket and ran after them. Her sides ached, and she could barely breathe by the time she pounded on Jenny's door.

She pushed her way past Mrs. Seker and found Jenny stretched out on the sofa. "I'm sorry," Carol said, stopping halfway across the room. "For everything. I want *you* for my friend, not Phoenix. And I already destroyed the Ouija board. What else can I do to get you to like me again?"

"I'm Sorry"

Jenny's face softened. She stared at Carol, thinking about what the girl had just said. "You don't need to do anything else. That's all I wanted."

"Then we can be friends again?"

Jenny nodded eagerly. Carol jumped over to her and hugged her. "Is there anything I can do to make you more comfortable?" she asked.

"Well, my favorite stuffed teddy bear is upstairs. The one you gave me."

"I'll get it!" Carol bounced up the steps and into Jenny's room. As she grabbed the bear off the bed, she spotted the gold top of a familiar frame in the trash can. Peering closer, she pulled it out.

As she handed the bear to Jenny, she held out the cracked photo of Jenny's father. "Why did you do this?" she asked.

"You know why," Jenny said, looking away.

"Why can't you forgive him the way you forgave me?"

"*You* said you were sorry. I don't think my dad was ever sorry about his stupid drinking problem."

"Why did you do this"

Carol studied the photo. "This broken glass makes him look evil," she remarked. "With new glass, maybe you could see him for the loving father he really was."

"What are you talking about?"

Carol explained. "Forgiving him would be like looking at him through new glass. If you forgive him, you can stop looking at the evil of his drinking problem and start seeing his love for you again."

"But he doesn't deserve my forgiveness."

"Do it for your own sake," Carol said. "It's no fun remembering only what he did wrong."

Jenny fell silent. It was hard to ignore the bitterness she felt, but she knew her friend was right. She longed to be able to remember her dad's love. "I want to forgive him" she said softly. "But God will have to help me. It still hurts."

Carol smiled at her. "Now that I've helped you solve your problem, will you help me solve mine?"

"Which is?"

"It still hurts"

"How can I get rid of that Ouija spirit?" She shoved aside some of the clutter on the coffee table to sit near Jenny.

"There's only one way. Jesus."

"Don't get overly religious on me," Carol moaned.

"You asked. The truth is, Jesus died on the cross to conquer evil, and that makes Him stronger than the Ouija spirit. So if you ask Jesus to fill your bedroom with His presence, the spirit won't be able to stay."

"Really?"

"But getting it out of your room isn't enough. You opened your life to the evil spirit by playing with the Ouija board. The only way to get it out of your life and keep it out is to have Jesus fill your life."

Carol shrugged. "How?"

"Well, by praying. I need to do this, too, because of when I played with the Ouija board." She closed her eyes. "Dear Jesus, forgive me for using

"There's only one way. Jesus."

the Ouija board. Forgive me for all my sins. I want You to fill my life with Your presence, Your love, Your peace, and Your victory over evil."

Carol repeated Jenny's prayer, then sighed deeply. "You know, Jen, I'd been feeling as if a scary blackness was surrounding me. Now I feel surrounded with—" She searched for the right word. "Peace."

Just then, both girls glanced at the wall near them. Their eyes had caught a glimpse of something shimmering, a white image that blended into the air and disappeared.

"Did you see that?" Carol asked.

"It looked like an—an angel."

"With a sword."

"Yeah," Jenny said with awe. "And I have the strong feeling it's protecting us."

"Me, too!"

It looked like an angel